AMELiA RULES!™

SUPERHEROES

Atheneum Books for Young Readers
New York   London   Toronto   Sydney

MEET THE GANG

Amelia Louise McBride:
Our heroine. Wise cracking, yet sweet. She spends her time hanging out with friends and her aunt Tanner.

Reggie Grabinsky:
A.k.a. Captain Amazing. Founder of G.A.S.P., which he forces . . . er, encourages, his friends to join.

Rhonda Bleenie:
Smart, stubborn, and loud. She wears her heart on her sleeve and it's filled with love for Reggie.

Pajamaman:
Never speaks. Always cool. His feetie jammies tell you what's on his mind.

Tanner:
Amelia's aunt and a former rock 'n' roll superstar.

Amelia's Mom (Mary):
Starting a new life in Pennsylvania with Amelia after the divorce.

Amelia's Dad:
Still lives in New York, and misses Amelia terribly.

G.A.S.P.
Gathering Of Awesome Super Pals. The superhero club Reggie founded.

Park View Terrace Ninjas:
Club across town and nemesis to G.A.S.P.

Kyle:
The main ninja. Kind of a jerk but not without charm.

Joan:
Former Park View Terrace Ninja (nemesis of G.A.S.P.), now friends with Amelia and company.

Tweenie Zeenie:

A local kid-run magazine and Web site.

ATHENEUM BOOKS FOR YOUNG READERS
An imprint of Simon & Schuster Children's Publishing Division
1230 Avenue of the Americas, New York, New York 10020

For information about special discounts for bulk purchases,
please contact Simon & Schuster Special Sales at 1-866-506-1949
or business@simonandschuster.com.

The Simon & Schuster Speakers Bureau can bring authors to your
live event. For more information or to book an event, contact
the Simon & Schuster Speakers Bureau at 1-866-248-3049
or visit our website at www.simonspeakers.com.

Book design by Sonia Chaghatzbanian
Manufactured in China
0612 GFC
First Atheneum Books for Young Readers
paperback edition January 2010
4 6 8 10 9 7 5 3
CIP data for this book is available
from the Library of Congress.
ISBN 978-1-4169-8606-5 (pbk)
These comics were originally published
individually by Renaissance Press.

To Major Stephen M. Murphy.
This book is for you, with thanks
for your service to our country,
and for your friendship.

Fireflies
and Time

IT'S WEIRD . . .

IN A WAY, I CAN'T BELIEVE FOURTH GRADE IS *OVER* . . . .

BUT ON THE OTHER HAND, I CAN'T BELIEVE IT TOOK SO LONG.

EVERY DAY YOU SIT IN CLASS, AND THE CLOCK SEEMS TO STAND STILL.

THEN ONE DAY YOU LOOK BEHIND YOU . . .

. . . AND WONDER WHERE ALL THE TIME WENT.

SUDDENLY, IN THE SMOKY GLOOM OF THE FOURTH-GRADE CLASSROOM THERE STANDS A FIGURE OF IMMENSE POWER.

NOT ALL WITNESSES WOULD LATER ATTEST THAT A CRY OF "UP, UP AND AWAY" WAS HEARD AS REGGIE SOARED SKYWARD, BUT MOST AGREE THERE WAS A HAND GESTURE.

"OEMAL!" THE MAGIC WORD NEEDED TO TURN INTO MIRACLE-REGGIE HAD BEEN FORGOTTEN FOR SO VERY LONG!

FLYING OUT OF HIS BORING 4TH-GRADE CLASSROOM, OUR HERO LEAPS INTO THE INFINITE!

SOARING THROUGH SPACE AND TIME, SPANNING COUNTLESS GALAXIES, MIRACLEREGGIE NOTES THAT ALTHOUGH THE UNIVERSE IS INFINITE, THERE ARE VERY FEW PLACES WHERE YOU CAN GET A DECENT BURRITO.

RATS.

MIRACLEREGGIE PAUSES TO REFLECT UPON THE BEAUTY OF PLANET QWXZIFM.
I BET CHICKS WOULD DIG A PINK PLANET, THINKS THE MAN OF MANY MIRACLES.

SUDDENLY...

MIRACLE REGGIE, YOUR DOOM IS AT HAND!

?!

OUT OF THE INKY BLACKNESS OF SPACE COMES MIRACLEREGGIE'S GREATEST FOES—THOSE MENACING MISCREANTS, *THE SPACE NINJAS!*

ATTACKED BY ASTRO ANARCHISTS! SUCKER-PUNCHED BY SPACE AGE PSYCHOPATHS! YET STILL THE MAN OF MIRACULOUS MIGHT *FIGHTS ON,* WAYLAYING HIS VILLAINOUS OPPONENTS WITH HIS FAMOUS *MIRACLE PUNCH!*

ALTHOUGH BADLY OUTNUMBERED, OUR BRAVE HERO *BATTLES!* THE SPACE NINJAS MAY WIN, THINKS THE BIG BLUE MARVEL, BUT AT LEAST THEY'LL EXPERIENCE MINOR ACHES AND PAINS!

BUT ALAS *EVEN VIRTUE* OF THE STRONGEST STRAIN MUST SUCCUMB AGAINST UNBELIEVABLE ODDS.

OUTNUMBERED, MIRACLEREGGIE IS UNABLE TO FEND OFF THE MALICIOUS MARAUDERS.

DESPERATE, THE TITAN OF TRUTH SENDS OUT A PSYCHIC CRY FOR HELP!

MIRACLEREGGIE'S PSYCHIC SIGNAL TRAVERSES THE VERY COSMOS ITSELF, FINDING ITS WAY TO A WATERY PLANET KNOWN TO US AS *EARTH!*

...AND THE EAR OF A FRIEND.

THERE IT FINDS ITS MARK IN A SMALL ALL-AMERICAN TOWN...

SUDDENLY, A MAGIC WORD IS SPOKEN AND A STRANGE (YET SOMEWHAT ATTRACTIVE) FIGURE ROCKETS INTO THE SKY!

THE SKY-BORNE SUPERBEING SHOOTS INTO THE STRATOSPHERE, LEAVING EARTHBOUND SPECTATORS STUNNED....

LOOK! UP IN THE SKY...

I DON'T WANNA!

WHY DO YOU HAVE TO BE SO DIFFICULT?!

MEANWHILE, MIRACLEREGGIE HAS LULLED HIS ATTACKERS INTO A FALSE SENSE OF SECURITY BY ALLOWING HIMSELF TO BE BEATEN BRUTALLY ABOUT THE FACE. THE SPACE NINJAS SEEM CERTAIN OF THEIR VICTORY, WHEN SUDDENLY...

BEWARE, VILLIANS, MIRACLETANNER IS HERE!

AND YOU'RE MESSING WITH MY MAN!

HOOOOOORAAY!!!

AND THAT WAS IT. GRADE FOUR.

JOE McCART ELEMENTA "Weeding out t wrong element since 1962"

THERE IS NOTHING IN THE WORLD LIKE THE LAST DAY OF SCHOOL.

I WISH I COULD DESCRIBE IT BETTER, BUT IT'S HARD, Y'KNOW?

IT KINDA FEELS LIKE IT'S SATURDAY MORNING, AND YOU HAVE A BOWL OF APPLE JACKS.

AND YOU'RE WATCHING CARTOONS AND IT'S ALL GOOD ONES....

AND THE CEREAL HAS MADE THE MILK ALL PINK AND SWEET....

AND MONDAY IS A HOLIDAY, AND IT'S GONNA SNOW ON TUESDAY, AND IT FEELS LIKE TIME IS STANDING STILL.

EHINDBAY THE AIRCHAY.

I SEE YOU, AMELIA!

HAHAHA HAHA

CHEATER!

THANK YOU, MISS TANNER.

NO SWEAT.

AND BESIDES, REGGIE ISN'T EXACTLY SOME SWASHBUCKLING HERO WHO'S GOING TO RESCUE YOU FROM HARM!

BUT RHONDA, I DON'T THINK IT'S GOOD FOR YOU TO PRETEND YOU'RE JUST SOME DAMSEL IN DISTRESS.
LIFE ISN'T AN OLD-FASHIONED MOVIE SERIAL, YOU KNOW.

VOICE-OVER: Once upon a time, in a distant land...

... there was an enchanted castle.

And in a tower, high above the castle walls, was a prisoner...

... the beautiful girl known only as Rhondapunzel.

RHONDAPUNZEL: Help! Help! I, Rhondapunzel, am trapped in this tower, and in need of rescuing. (Eligible princes only need apply.)

REGINALD: Hark! What doth cometh on yon morn breeze? Zounds! 'Tis the cry of a hot chick in distress!

OOH! HE LOOKS SO DREAMY ON THE BIG SCREEN.

REGINALD: Fear not, fair hottie! For Reginald of the Woods is here! Lower your hair and I shall climb up to rescue you anon!

SFX: (Whip Whip Whip)

SFX: (Sproing!)
RHONDAPUNZEL: How embarrassing!

SFX: (Tug Tug)

REGINALD: Huff! Huff!

RHONDAPUNZEL: Ouch! Ouch!

REGINALD: Take heart, fair maiden! For I, Reginald of the Woods, have come to save you.

RHONDAPUNZEL: I knew that if I waited long enough, a handsome prince would come to rescue me.

RHONDAPUNZEL: You ARE a prince, aren't you?

REGINALD: Well, not exactly, but my dad has most of his albums.

RHONDAPUNZEL: Close enough!

SFX: Smooooooooooooooch!!

WOO HOO

REGINALD: Hmmm...I just thought of something.
RHONDAPUNZEL: Yes, my love?

REGINALD: Now that I've rescued you, who is gonna rescue me?

17

RHONDA?

OH, NEVER MIND.

OH, KIDS...

I HAVE A SURPRISE FOR ANY AND ALL FOURTH-GRADE GRADUATES.

IS IT A TOY?

IS IT A GAME?

IS IT A CAT?

IS IT CASH?

IS IT A DOG?

I'D LIKE CASH!

DOES IT HAVE PINEAPPLE ON IT? PINEAPPLE PIZZA RULES!

IF YOU'D LIKE TO ADOPT A SON, I THINK SOMETHING COULD BE ARRANGED.

YOU SAVED ME FROM A NIGHT OF FISH STICKS AND ASPARAGUS.

THE NIGHT WAS AWESOME. IT FELT GREAT NOT TO WORRY ABOUT SCHOOL OR MY PARENTS OR ANYTHING.

I ONCE READ ABOUT A FIELD NOT FAR FROM HERE . . . .

EVERY SUMMER IT'S FILLED WITH LIGHTNING BUGS THAT ALL FLASH IN UNISON.

SCIENTISTS DON'T KNOW WHY . . . BUT I ALWAYS THOUGHT . . .

. . . THE FIREFLIES WERE TRYING TO TELL US SOMETHING.

ACK.

:giggle!:

AND WHEN IT WAS TIME FOR EVERYONE TO GO, WE WENT OUTSIDE AND THERE WERE ALL THESE FIREFLIES.

THEY WERE EVERYWHERE. IT WAS REALLY BEAUTIFUL.

AND I'M NOT SURE WHY, BUT IT WAS ALSO KINDA SAD.

LET'S GET 'EM!

20

LATER THAT NIGHT . . .

I HAD A DREAM.

IT TOOK A WHILE FOR ME TO REALIZE THAT IT WAS JUST
A DREAM   AND THAT IT WAS MORNING NOW, AND
THAT I WAS SAFE AND THAT EVERYTHING WAS OKAY.

Into
Graceland

MOVING?

AT FIRST I JUST FIGURED
    I *HEARD* HER WRONG.

MAYBE SHE SAID
SOMETHING THAT
RHYMED WITH "MOVING"....

LIKE...
UM...

NOT "*MOVING*," SHE
COULDN'T
HAVE SAID THAT!

BOOVING? NO
COOVING? NO
DOOVING? NO
EOOVING? NO
FOOVING? NO

GROOVING!
THAT'S IT!
WE ARE
TOTALLY
GROOVING!

CAN YOU
FEEL
IT?

IT WASN'T ALL BAD NEWS, I GUESS. I MEAN, IT WASN'T LIKE WE WERE MOVING TO MARS OR ANYTHING. THE HOUSE WAS IN PARK VIEW TERRACE, WHICH IS JUST ACROSS TOWN. THE PROBLEM WAS, THOUGH, IT WAS A WHOLE DIFFERENT SCHOOL DISTRICT. AND IT SEEMED TOO FAR FOR ME TO SEE MY FRIENDS. AT LEAST NOT ALL THE TIME LIKE WE WERE USED TO.

CONNERTON

GREENBELT

INTERSTATE 61

PARK VIEW TERRACE

WHEN I TOLD THEM, MY FRIENDS TOOK IT PRETTY BAD.

REGGIE LOOKED FUNNY, A LITTLE BIT LIKE A FROG THAT ATE A REALLY SPICY FLY.

PAJAMAMAN HAD A MELTDOWN, WHICH WAS FLATTERING, BUT MAYBE A LITTLE EXTREME.

AND RHONDA, WELL, I GUESS RHONDA'S REACTION WAS MIXED.

ROCKER

MOVING?

31

MOM, OF COURSE, WAS SUPEREXCITED AND SHE DIDN'T SEEM TO NOTICE THAT I WASN'T.

I WAS PRETTY SURE NO ONE DID.

AND THE NEXT THING YOU KNOW, IT WAS MOVING DAY.

I PROPOSE THAT PM AND I FORGET THE LIFTING...

...AND TAKE GUARD DUTY.

OH, AND THIS HAS NOTHING TO DO WITH TRYING TO GET OUT OF WORK?

NO WAY, AMELIA. SECURITY IS A REAL ISSUE.

SCENARIO...

IT'S HOT... EVERYONE'S LIFTING HEAVY STUFF....

oh BROTHER!

EVERYONE GOES INSIDE FOR A COOL, TASTY BEVERAGE.

LEAVING THE TRUCK UNATTENDED.

THE PERFECT CHANCE FOR A ROUGE SUPERVILLIAN TO ATTACK!

REGGIE, I DON'T HAVE TIME. RHONDA JUST BROKE ANOTHER —

Good example! Are you sure Rhonda is on our side?

She could be a double agent trying to sabotage this mission.

You need superhero protection.

YOU JUST WANT TO GET OUT OF WORKING...

...AND STILL BE THANKED LIKE THE REST OF US.

THAT IS NOT TRUE!

SUPERHEROES NEVER NEED TO BE THANKED!

OH, HE JUST WANTS TO READ THAT COMIC BOOK IN HIS POCKET.

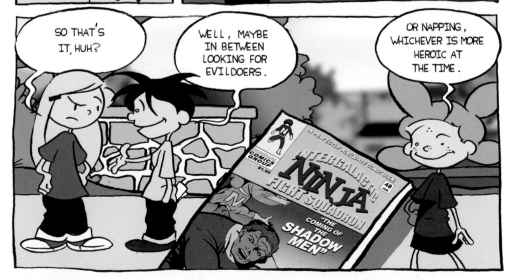

SO THAT'S IT, HUH?

WELL, MAYBE IN BETWEEN LOOKING FOR EVILDOERS.

OR NAPPING, WHICHEVER IS MORE HEROIC AT THE TIME.

A PERFECTLY ABSOLUTELY COMICS BOOK

INTERGALACTIC NINJA FIGHT SQUADRON

COMICS GROUP $1.95

48 JUN.

"THE COMING OF THE SHADOW MEN"

I'VE BEEN WAITING TO READ THIS THING FOR WEEKS!

IT'S A COOL BOOK, IT JUST NEVER COMES OUT ON TIME.

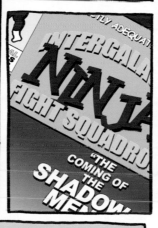

I THINK THE ARTIST HAS "ISSUES".

LAST ISSUE, THE SQUADRON WAS CAPTURED BY THE SHADOW MEN.

TANK! PEE-WEE! DON'T! YOU'RE PLAYING RIGHT INTO THE SHADOW LORD'S EVIL TRAP!

HONESTLY, IT'S LOOKING PRETTY BAD FOR THEM.

NOOOOOO!!

>HEE HEE< TANK AND PEE-WEE ARE SUCH MORONS!

THINK ABOUT IT... PEOPLE FAMOUS FOR DOING NOTHING...

... MAKING FUN OF PEOPLE TRYING TO DO SOMETHING...

...TO ENTERTAIN PEOPLE WHO WILL NEVER DO ANYTHING.

AND YOUR POINT IS?

AMERICAN IDOL IS THE WORK OF THE DEVIL.

YOU ARE TOTALLY MESSED UP.

SO I'VE HEARD.

SO THIS IS PARK VIEW TERRACE?

SO, UH, DO NINJAS ED AND KYLE LIVE AROUND HERE?

RIGHT DOWN THE BLOCK IN THAT RANCHER.

ER... NOT...NOT THAT I CARE.

MM HMM.

NOBODY SAY A WORD.

OOH, KYLE! ARE YOU OKAY? THAT LOOKED WICKED PAINFUL.

I'M FINE.

UH, KYLE? IF YOU'RE OKAY, MAYBE WE SHOULD GET ROLLING. I'M A LITTLE WORRIED...

...ABOUT OUR ISSIONMAY?

ISSIONMAY?

YOU KNOW, THE EGIONLAY OF EVESSTAY.

OH, IGHTRAY! THE EGIONLAY! I ALMOST ORGOTFAY.

IF WE URRYHAY WE IGHTMAY STILL ATCHCAY EMTHAY.

WHO'S THE LEGION OF STEVES?

Leg..uh...

OH! umm...

I OLDTAY OUYAY OTNAY OTAY ALKTAY BOUTAY ECRETSAY INJANAY UFFSTAY EARNAY OTENTIALPAY INJANAY IVALSRAY! OUYAY OOFUSDAY!

THEY OBVIOUSLY EAKSPAY IGPAY ATINLAY.

THEN WHY ARE YOU STILL SPEAKING IT, YOU ERKJAY?

I HAVE TONS OF BOYFRIENDS (ZACK, SEAN, SNAKE, STICKPIN), BUT FOR SOME REASON MOM HATES ALL OF THEM.

THEN SHE TOTALLY FREAKS WHEN, ON MY SIXTEENTH BIRTHDAY, I COME HOME WITH A BELLY BUTTON RING.

THINGS GET BAD AND I MOVE BACK TO NEW YORK TO BE WITH DAD. HE'S COOL, BUT I SPEND MOST OF MY TIME IN CLUBS, DOWN IN THE VILLAGE.

ONE NIGHT, YEARS AFTER LEAVING PENNSYLVANIA, I RUN INTO PAJAMAMAN. HE'S PLAYING BASS IN SOME BAND. WE HAVE A BRIEF THING. IT DOESN'T WORK OUT.

A COUPLE OF YEARS LATER I'M TEMPING AT SOME OFFICE. I GOOGLE THE NAME REGGIE GRABINSKY, BUT THERE ARE NO MATCHES.

48

SO IT'S NICE. A LITTLE OLD-LADYISH, BUT...

RAGILE

...Y'KNOW, A FEW COATS OF PAINT AND IT'LL BE TOTALLY GROOVIN'!

OH YEAH, IT'S A REGULAR GRACELAND.

YEP, PUT A PINK CAR IN THIS ROOM AND YOU'LL NEVER REGRET MOVING IN.

HEY, I ALREADY DON'T REGRET MOVING IN.

I HAD THE BEST REASON IN THE WORLD.

TANNER KNEW WHAT MOVING WOULD MEAN TO ME. SHE KNEW HOW BADLY IT WOULD MAKE ME FEEL.

SHE NEVER SAID THAT WAS WHY SHE DECIDED TO TAKE THE HOUSE INSTEAD OF MOM, BUT I KNEW.

I KNEW.

JUST LAST YEAR SHE OPENED UP HER HOUSE TO ME AND MOM, AND NOW SHE WAS GIVING IT UP ALTOGETHER, JUST FOR ME.

AND NOW I'M STANDING HERE, AND MOM IS IN THE CAR....

SHE'S WAITING TO TAKE ME BACK HOME....

BACK TO OUR HOME, BUT I DON'T WANT TO MOVE MY FEET...

I WANT TO SAY SOMETHING TO TANNER, BUT I CAN'T THINK OF ANYTHING.

SO I RUN BACK IN AND
I JUMP UP ON HER AND
I'M HUGGING HER AROUND
HER NECK AND I START
CRYING AND SHE STARTS
LAUGHING AND I
STILL CAN'T THINK
OF ANYTHING TO SAY.

BUT IT DOESN'T MATTER,
CUZ SUPERHEROES
NEVER NEED TO BE
THANKED ANYWAY.

Old Friends
Who Just Met

SUMMER WAS GETTING WEIRD...

AFTER WE FOUND REGGIE AND PAJAMAMAN TIED TO THAT TREE, IT SEEMED LIKE REGGIE BECAME **OBSESSED** WITH THE NINJAS. PLUS THERE WAS SOME NEW GROUP CALLED THE **LEGION OF STEVES** THAT HE WAS ALWAYS RANTING ABOUT.

TWO WEEKS PASSED SINCE TANNER HAD MOVED OUT, AND EVEN THOUGH SHE WAS JUST ACROSS TOWN, I WAS REALLY **MISSING** HER. AND BECAUSE I'M APPARENTLY A MORON, I DECIDED TO DISCUSS MY FEELINGS WITH **RHONDA**...

KID LIGHTNING, I GIVE YOU THE NEW **AMAZING MOBILE**....THE MOST **POWERFUL** CRIME-FIGHTING VEHICLE SEEN SINCE I DROVE THE LAST AMAZING MOBILE OFF THAT CLIFF.

WITH IT, WE WILL INVADE THE NINJAS' **HEADQUARTERS** AND DISCOVER WHAT THEY KNOW ABOUT THIS MYSTERIOUS "LEGION OF STEVES."

IT'S REALLY THE **LITTLE** THINGS THAT I MISS THE MOST, Y'KNOW? LIKE SHE USED TO PLAY HER GUITAR UP IN THE ATTIC.

PERHAPS THEY WILL BE OUR ALLIES IN OUR STRUGGLE AGAINST THE NINJAS. FOR LIKE THE OLD SAYING GOES...

Mmmm-Hmm

THE AMAZING MOBILE

RHONDA AND I HAD OPTED OUT OF REGGIE'S LATEST *G. A. S. P** OPERATION AND DECIDED TO VISIT TANNER IN HER NEW HOUSE. IT WAS A LONG BIKE RIDE, BUT IT BEAT TRAVELING IN THE *AMAZING MOBILE*. BETWEEN MY HOUSE AND PARK VIEW TERRACE IS A ROAD CALLED *THE GREENBELT*. IT'S A NATURE TRAIL THAT'S ONLY FOR, LIKE, BIKES AND WALKING AND STUFF.

*Gathering of
Awesome Super Pals

IT'S *BEAUTIFUL* AND
FUN TO RIDE ON, AND ALL...

...BUT FOR A
NEW YORK GIRL,
IT'S A LITTLE *TOO
MUCH* GREEN,
YA KNOW?

BY THE TIME WE
GOT TO TANNER'S
I WAS READY FOR
SOME *CIVILIZATION*.

EVER MEET SOMEBODY, AND YOU'RE EXCITED CUZ YOU THINK YOU KNOW THEM? BUT THEN YOU REALIZE YOU DON'T? BUT THEN THEY ACT LIKE THEY KNOW YOU? AND THERE'S THAT WEIRD MOMENT OF SILENCE? ISN'T THAT AWKWARD?

WELL, THIS WAS LIKE THAT. . . ANYWAY. . .

KOFF KOFF

~AHEM~ EXCUSE ME!

C'MON . . .

WE'RE HANGING OUT OUT BACK.

WE SHOULD'VE FIGURED YOU'D SHOW UP HERE.

HEY, AMELIA. LONG TIME NO SEE.

UH . . . YEAH. GOOD TO . . . RIGHT . . . YEAH.

YOU DON'T REMEMBER US, DO YOU?

I WAS WRACKING MY BRAIN, BUT I JUST COULDN'T *PLACE* THEM.

EVEN WHEN THEY GAVE AN *NC-17 HINT*.

A MONKEY!

NO, A CHICKEN!

A CHKKEN DATING A MONKEY!

NO, A MONKEY KISSING A...

oh, yeah.

RIGHT!

IT WAS TRISH AND JOANNE, EYEWITNESSES TO THE GREAT *NINJA SMOOCHIE INCIDENT*. THEY RELAYED THE STORY IN GORY DETAIL TO THE OTHER KID, SAM.

WHILE I WAS BECOMING THE *FOUNDING MOTHER* OF MY OWN *HUMILIATION NATION*....

SUDDENLY I COULDN'T WAIT FOR TANNER TO GET HOME.

DON'T TOUCH ANYTHING UNLESS YOU HAVE TO.

NINJA COOTIES HAVE BEEN KNOWN TO KILL.

WAIT A SECOND, WHAT'S THIS?

HEY! IT'S MY *NINJA FIGHT SQUADRON* COMIC

THOSE JERKS STOLE IT!

IS NOTHING SACRED?

AHA! THIS IS IT!

A WHOLE FILE DEDICATED TO STEVES.

THIS'LL TEACH US ALL WE NEED TO...

...KNOW?

AND SPEAKING OF *PAINS IN THE BUTT*. . .I FIGURED THE BEST WAY TO STOP BEING EMBARRASSED WAS TO START DOING THE EMBARRASSING. SO I TURNED THE SPOTLIGHT ON MY GOOD FRIEND RHONDA.

I DON'T GET IT.

OH, C'MON!

LOOK! IT'S JOAN!

HEY, JOAN!

OH, LOOK, A *GIRL NINJA* WE CAN HANG WITH.

Y'KNOW, FOR WHEN WE'RE NOT BEING *SUPERHEROES*.

VERY HEALTHY.

OKAY, RHONDA HAD A POINT, Y'KNOW? AND I COULD JUST IMAGINE WHAT *REGGIE* WOULD SAY.

BUT THE THING IS, SHE SEEMED *PRETTY COOL!* IN FACT, SHE WAS *HILARIOUS*. LIKE THIS...

SO HOW'S LIFE IN THE *NINJAS?* HOW WAS THE *INITIATION?*

OH, Y'KNOW, IT WAS ALL RIGHT.

I PASSED ALL THE TRIALS.

Y'KNOW, SPITTING, SWEARING, NORWEGIAN PINKY WRESTLING...

BUT WHEN THE MEETING'S OVER, THEY ALL TAKE OFF...

...AND TELL ME I CAN'T COME ALONG.

Y'KNOW, "NO GIRLS ALLOWED."

SO I WAS REALLY TICKED OFF, Y'KNOW?

I MEAN, I'VE BEEN A DIE-HARD *FEMINIST* SINCE AGE FIVE.

SO I FOLLOW THEM INTO THE WOODS, AND I HEAR THIS *LAUGHING* AND *SPLASHING*, SO I PEEK OUT FROM THE BUSHES... AND GOT THE *SHOCK* OF MY LIFE.

WHAT?!

WHAT WAS IT?!

WHAT DID YOU GET?

I GOT THE FULL NINJA.

OH, YES.

AH HAHAHAHAHAHA

YOU'RE **KIDDING!**

NUH-UH! THEY WERE N-U-D-E NAKED, AND SWIMMING IN THIS POND.

SO I GET AN EYEFUL OF THIS SCENE, AND, LIKE, TOTALLY FREAK. *"AAAAGH! MY EYES! MY EYES!"*

SO THEY ALL GO RUNNING BEHIND THIS SHRUB, SREAMING, *"GET OUT OF HERE! GET OUT!"*

WAIT A SECOND, IF THEY WERE IN THE WATER AND THEN BEHIND A SHRUB, YOU DIDN'T **REALLY** SEE ANYTHING...RIGHT?

WEEELL...

IT WAS A VERY **SMALL** SHRUB.

WHY DON'T I GIVE YOU A MINUTE TO ERASE THAT HORRIBLE IMAGE. OKAY, READY? LET'S CONTINUE.
WE ENDED UP HANGING OUT FOR A LONG TIME, AND IT WAS KINDA COOL. JOAN WAS EASILY THE MOST
NORMAL NINJA I'D MET YET, AND EVERYONE ELSE SEEMED NICE TOO. SO WHEN NINJA JOAN HAD TO GO
HOME, WE DIDN'T MIND BEING HIJACKED OVER TO JOANNE'S HOUSE.

THE REASON JOANNE WANTED US TO
COME OVER WAS TO SHOW US HER
MAGAZINE, THE *TWEENIE ZEENIE*.
IT WAS TOTALLY WEIRD. JOANNE
PUBLISHED THIS LITTLE BOOK OFF
HER HOME COMPUTER AND SOLD IT
TO KIDS IN THE NEIGHBORHOOD. IT
WAS NEAT, I GUESS. IT HAD
STORIES AND PICTURES AND
EVEN A LITTLE *GOSSIP
COLUMN*. THE LATEST ISSUE
WAS A SPECIAL ALL-NINJA
EXTRAVAGANZA AND FEATURED
AN INTERVIEW WITH KYLE AND
JOAN. THE GOSSIP COLUMN
SAID THEY WERE AN *ITEM*, BUT
A NINJA SPOKESMAN DENIED IT.

SAM DID ALL THE ILLUSTRATIONS, AND HE WAS PRETTY GOOD.
THE INSIDE COVER LISTED FIVE WRITERS (INCLUDING
WILLIAM BIRCHBEER, LEO TOLLBOOTH, AND *ERNIE HAMWAY*),
BUT IT TURNS OUT THEY WERE ALL TRISHIA. SHE WROTE
THE GOSSIP COLUMN AND A SPORTS REPORT AND A WHOLE
BUNCH OF OTHER STUFF ON JOANNE'S COMPUTER. BUT IN
THE BACK OF EVERY ISSUE WAS A STORY CALLED THE
ADVENTURES OF PRINCESS TRISHARA. THAT STORY TRISHIA
WAS WRITING BY HAND IN A BIG LEATHER BOOK.
IT WAS THE ONLY THING IN THE MAGAZINE
THAT TRISHIA SIGNED HER REAL NAME TO.

BUT WHILE RHONDA SAWED LOGS, I READ EVERY CHAPTER OF *TRISHARA*. I GOTTA ADMIT, I WAS KINDA READING IT CUZ I THOUGHT IT MIGHT BE *MOCKABLE*. BUT IT WAS COOL. REALLY, REALLY COOL, IN FACT. THERE WERE WIZARDS AND FAIRIES AND DRAGONS AND Y'KNOW... *OH MY*!

HOW CAN YOU TAKE SOMEONE *SERIOUSLY* WHEN THEY SPEND HALF THEIR LIFE PRETENDING TO BE SOMETHING OUT OF A *COMIC BOOK*?

NOW, RHONDA, DON'T TELL ME YOU HAVE A CASE OF *NINJA FEVER*?

ME? NO! OF *COURSE NOT!*

ARE YOU KIDDING? SHE'S GOT A MAJOR THING FOR THIS WEIRD FRIEND OF OURS.

OOOOOH! A *BOYFRIEND!* DO YOU LET HIM *SMOOCH* YOU PASSIONATELY?

EEW GROSS!

ERT

No, he's not *really* my boyfriend, but he is *sweet* and *talented* and really *smart*.

She may be...um... *exaggerating* a little.

He's the most *wonderful boy* in the world.

And even though he's never said so, I'm *sure* he feels the same *about me*.

If we keep hanging out, maybe you'll get to *meet him* someday.

ATTENTION CITIZENS

78

My Novel's Gonna Need an Evil Villain

...ORDER!

Gimme that BACK!

You ROTTEN, LOUSY NO GOOD —

OWEN!

I'M THE CLUB PRESIDENT! SHOW SOME RESPECT!!

CLUB PRESIDENT?!

Isn't the whole POINT of this club to overthrow society's RULES and bring about ANARCHY?

NO, ACTUALLY, IT'S NOT.

Oh...

My bad.

NOW CAN WE PLEASE GET SERIOUS? WHILE WE GOOF AROUND, THE LEGION OF STEVES IS NO DOUBT PLOTTING SOMETHING DASTARDLY.

WHAT'S ALL THIS MUMBO JUMBO ABOUT THE LEGION OF STEVES? WHO ARE THEY?

WHO ARE THE LEGION OF STEVES?

WELL, ULTRA VIOLET...

UNDERSTANDING

STEVES

HI. I'M **CAPTAIN AMAZING.**

FOR SOME TIME NOW, I'VE BEEN WORKING TO STAMP OUT EVIL.

BUT UNTIL RECENTLY, I BELIEVED THAT EVIL WAS A **RANDOMLY OCCURRING PHENOMENON.**

AND **NOT** THE RESULT OF A SINGLE ORGANIZATION OR GROUP.

HOWEVER, NEW INFORMATION HAS REVEALED THAT, IN FACT, ALL OF THE **EVIL,** ALL OF THE **SUFFERING,** ALL OF THE **GENERAL POOPINESS** THAT OCCURS ANYWHERE IN THE WORLD...

...IS CAUSED BY GUYS NAMED **STEVE.**

UH-OH.

ALLOW ME TO ELABORATE.

83

*Some experts doubt the authenticity of these documents, citing the fact that they were written on Post-its, and contain several oblique references to Chicken McNuggets.

*Actually, this chart makes no sense, but it always looks more official when you have a chart.

See, the thing about Sarah is, she was, well, very Sarah-ish, you know? She totally was her own person. She wanted to be a writer, so she wrote. And those Lucy and Mew books were superpopular. When I was a kid, they made Softee Chicken look pretty much like…well, like Softee Chicken. But Sarah didn't want to be famous. That's why she used the pen name. Some people knew her for years and never knew what she did.

Now, here's the interesting part. When she was just twenty and living in New York City, Sarah met her one true love, another aspiring writer named Hugh S. Travers. They were inseparable. Everything was perfect except that the better Sarah's career went, the worse Hugh's did. Still, that didn't stop their love. They lived a very New York life—same street, different buildings. Together when they wanted, apart when they needed.

And they vowed never to get married.

So everything's going along normally. Sarah's selling zillions of books. Hugh's collecting rejection slips. Then one day Hugh's mother gets sick. Really sick. Hugh needs to go back to Pennsylvania, to the town where he grew up, to take care of her. So, on the night before he leaves, he does the unthinkable and asks Sarah to marry him. Of course, she says no. Hugh is heartbroken, but he has responsibilities and leaves New York, never to return.

Five years pass. Sarah has no contact with Hugh, but she never forgets him. She writes another book called *Lucy and Mew: Against Unbelievable Odds*. It's totally a mash note to Hugh, but written so that only he would understand. Sarah has no idea if he'll ever see it. He does. He gets it. They reconnect, and it's still magic.

She moves to Pennsylvania. To Hugh's hometown. To this TOWN. She buys this house, and they live happily ever after. Unmarried, on the same street and in two different houses.

When Hugh died, Sarah didn't spend much time here, but she kept the house.

I moved here in large part to be near Sarah. My sister moved here to stay with me, and she brought Amelia along with her.

AND NOW, HERE WE ARE.

DID HUGH EVER GET ANY BOOKS PUBLISHED?

YEAH, EVENTUALLY. HE WROTE THE SPOINGLE BOOKS UNDER THE NAME *PROFESSOR SCHMUTZ*.

89

I'M JUST THINKING OF ALL WE DO FOR LOVE.

REGGIE, EVEN THOUGH YOU'RE CRAZY, I WANT YOU TO KNOW I SUPPORT YOU.

THANKS, RHONDA. NOW, LOOK.

THAT STEVE OVER THERE WAS MENTIONED IN THE NINJA'S FILES. I'M GONNA CHECK HIM OUT.

THE REST OF YOU...

...JUST ACT COOL.

BE CAREFUL, YOU BRAVE, WONDERFUL BOY, YOU.

I WILL.

OH, SHUT UP.

90

91

LOOK OUTSIDE. IT'S YOUR FRIENDS.

WOW. IS... IS THAT NORMAL?

YOU MEAN THE CHAOS, THE VIOLENCE, THE UNDERWEAR?

KRASH!

YEAH. *SIGH.* THAT'S NORMAL.

AT LEAST NO ONE *SNEEZE BARFED* YET.

I'M GONNA GO AHEAD AND IGNORE THAT STATEMENT.

LET ME IN. I'M DESERTING.

BOOKS

TANNER CLARK

OH, NICE VISUAL. VERY ATTRACTIVE.

PUCKER UP AND SMOOCH IT, McBRIDE.

AND GRACEFUL, TOO.

WHOA WAM!

WHAT'S GOING ON OUT THERE?

OH, SOMETHING ABOUT REGGIE FIGHTING THE LEAGUE OF KEVINS OR SOMETHING.

AND YOU'RE A PART OF IT?

HEY, I STAND BY MY MAN EVEN WHEN HE'S STANDING IN OZ.

OOOH, ICE CREAM!

YIKES! GOOD THING PM WEARS THAT HELMET.

LOOK OVER THERE!

YOWZA! WHY IS MARY VIOLET TRYING TO REMOVE THAT GUY'S CRANIUM?

HE'S LIKE THE HEAD TODD OR SOMETHING.

I DUNNO... IT'S PRETTY CONFUSING.

SO, ARE WE WINNING?

UMM...

WHAT'S the FREQUENCY, STEVE?!

YAAH!

WOO

IT'S KINDA HARD TO TELL.

WELL, YOU'LL NEVER SEE ME IN THAT STUPID CLUB OF YOURS!

IT'S WAY TOO FREAKY.

NEVER SAY NEVER.

ENOUGH!!

OKAY, YOU LITTLE WEIRDOS. I DON'T KNOW WHAT'S UP YOUR UNDIES!

(WHICH, BY THE WAY, ARE TRADITIONALLY WORN INSIDE THE PANTS!)

BUT I AM SICK OF THIS!!

EVER SINCE I STARTED DATING JULIE, I HAD TA DEAL WITH THOSE BRATS IN SKI MASKS!

FINE.

BUT THERE IS NO WAY I'M GONNA BE MAULED...

...BY the AVENGE NERDS.

NOW I GOT ONE THING TO SAY...

96

IF I EVER CATCH YOU...

POK!

TAKE THAT, EVIL STEVE!

AND PREPARE TO FACE THE WRATH...

...OF THE PARK VIEW TERRACE NINJAS.

POP!

IT'S THE END OF THE LINE, STEVIE BOY.

FIRE AT WILL, NINJA JOAN.

OH BOY. THIS IS GONNA BE FUN.

DID YOU **SEE** the **LOOK** on **STEVE'S** **FACE?!** *"HAHA"* IT WAS all *ÄÄÄÄGH!* HEE HEE HEE

WE MAKE A GOOD TEAM!

WE SURE DO! IT'S LIKE THAT OLD SAYING, MY BEST ENEMY IS MY FRIEND...

NO, WAIT...

OKAY, WE **GOT** IT!!

WHY DON'T YOU CHECK ON THE SITUATION?

OKAY. HANG ON.

IS EVERYTHING **OKAY** **DOWN THERE?**

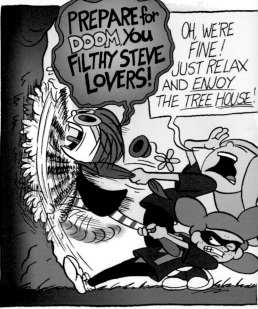

PREPARE for **DOOM,** YOU **FILTHY STEVE LOVERS!**

OH, WE'RE FINE! JUST RELAX AND *ENJOY* THE *TREE HOUSE!*

EVENTUALLY MARY VIOLET CALMED DOWN AND EVERYONE WENT HOME.

I DIDN'T SEE MUCH OF THOSE GUYS OVER THE NEXT FEW DAYS.

TRISH AND I WERE SPENDING ALL OUR TIME ON THE GREENBELT, READING ABOUT SARAH AND LUCY AND MEW AND ESPECIALLY PROFESSOR SCHMUTZ.

A Spoingle in Full

I never should have tasted
The bright blue caviar.
I should've known I hated
Monkey buttocks in a jar.
I ate the moldy sushi
Offered by my old pal Zack.
Now will you please excuse me?
I think I'm gonna yak.

THAT'S NOT A RELATIVE.

HE ALMOST WAS, THOUGH, BY MARRIAGE, ANYWAY.

I GUESS.

WOW.

THAT'S ONE FREAKY RELATIVE YOU HAD.

TOO BAD HE'S NOT ALIVE. YOU COULD ASK HIM ABOUT THIS:

A Spoingle BETRAYED!

Spoingle loves the wozzle
Wozzle loves a flea.
I really dig the spoingle
But Spongie can't stand me.
So I'll just talk to Fleeber
Whose eyes are glowing red
And see if he'll come over
To STEP ON FLEA BAG'S HEAD.

HE WAS MY GREAT AUNT'S BOYFRIEND.

I THINK GOOD OL' HUGH MAY HAVE HAD SOME JEALOUSY ISSUES.

SOUNDS LIKE IT.

101

TELL ME AGAIN WHY I'M DRESSED LIKE A SPAZ.

YOU COULDA BEEN A NINJA, BUT NO.

THE COSTUME INSTILLS FEAR INTO EVILDOERS, TRISH. IT'S ESSENTIAL.

TWANG

OOPS!

Are my WINGS on straight?

ED

NINJA KYLE

HOW DO POLKA-DOT BOXERS INSTILL FEAR, EXACTLY?

HE DOESN'T WASH THEM. GET CLOSER, YOU'LL BE AFRAID.

P.U.

NINJA JOAN

NINJA JOAN

NINJA JOAN

SMASH

UMM... I THINK NOW WOULD BE A GOOD TIME TO START OUR NEXT MISSION.

HUH? OH, OKAY.

NINJA KYLE

DON'T WORRY, TRISH, FIGHTING EVIL IS FUN. JUST WAIT AND SEE!

NINJA JOAN

SOMEDAY, WHEN I'M, LIKE, THIRTY AND ALL BROKEN DOWN AND DECREPIT AND I'M LOOKING BACK AT THE PAST, TRYING TO FIGURE OUT WHAT DAY WAS THE FUNNEST, THIS DAY WILL *TOTALLY* BE A CONTENDER.

WE ALL WENT TO THE PARK AND JUST PLAYED. WE PLAYED *FREEZE* TAG AND *HIDE AND GO SEEK* . . . EVERYTHING! IT WAS PERFECT.

UNTIL . . .

WHAT'S GOING ON?

WHAT'S GOING ON? DID ANYONE EVER TELL YOU THAT YOU'RE A TROUBLEMAKER, LITTLE GIRL?

EVERYBODY TELLS ME THAT.

WHAT'S GOING ON?

HE DIDN'T ANSWER ME. HE JUST OPENED THE CAR DOOR AND TRISH GOT IN.

SHE DIDN'T SAY ANYTHING, EITHER.

SHE JUST LOOKED . . .

HELPLESS, I GUESS.

AND KINDA SCARED.

AND THEN THEY WERE GONE.

AFTER THAT, NO ONE SAW TRISHIA FOR WEEKS.

IT RAINED OFF AND ON, WHICH ALWAYS STINKS DURING SUMMER VACATION.

ONE DAY JOANNE
SHOWED UP WITH
THE NEW *TWEENIE ZEENIE*.
EVERYONE WANTED TO KNOW
WHAT HAPPENED TO
PRINCESS TRISHARA.

ESPECIALLY ME.

I WAS SPENDING A LOT OF TIME AT TANNER'S. THERE WAS A COOL LITTLE BEDROOM IN THE BACK OF THE HOUSE THAT I CLAIMED. FROM THE WINDOW, I COULD SEE TRISH'S HOUSE.

I SAW HER DAD COMING AND GOING. I SAW HER MOM IN THE YARD GARDENING.

BUT I NEVER SAW TRISH.

THEN ONE NIGHT I WAS STAYING AT TANNER'S.

AT FIRST I THOUGHT I IMAGINED IT.

BUT FROM ACROSS THE YARD I COULD MAKE OUT TRISH. SHE WAS IN HER ROOM.

SHE WAS SHINING A LIGHT IN LITTLE BURSTS, LIKE MORSE CODE.

OR LIKE A FIREFLY...

...THAT WAS TRYING TO TELL ME SOMETHING.

When the Hero
Takes a Fall

IT'S CALLED A VENTRICULAR SEPTAL DEFECT.

I DON'T KNOW MUCH ABOUT IT.

Luann

WOW. BRAVE.

FAVORITE CARTOON?

SOFTEE CHICKEN.

FAVORITE DRINK?

DANGER MOUSE. YOURS?

EGG

BUT I GUESS IT'S SERIOUS.

A CHOCO SODA. IT'S GOOD!

EGG CREAM! EEW! WHAT'S THAT? IT SOUNDS GROSS!

LOOK, AMELIA...

OH YEAH. SHE'S THE EVIL ANTI-TANNER.

WHAT'S YOURS?

GRAPE TANG.

I'M SORRY TO HAVE TO TELL YOU THIS.

I DON'T MEAN TO TURN YOUR WORLD ON ITS EAR.

112

I CAN'T BELIEVE SHE ADMITTED IT!

WE WERE ONLY JOKING!

DOES SHE KNOW? ARE YOU GONNA TELL HIM? DO YOU THINK HE LIKES YOU BACK? HAVE YOU EVER HELD HANDS? HAVE YOU EVER KISSED?

KISS? ONCE... SORTA.

HOLY COW! DID *HE* KISS *YOU?*

NO.

YOU KISSED *HIM?!*

only to make up for kissing Kyle.

WOW! YOU ARE A TOTAL BIMBO!

I AM *NOT* A BIMBO!

YES YOU ARE! YOU'RE BETTY BIMBO!

Fine. I'm BETTY BIMBO. Can we PLEASE DROP it?!

SURE, BETTY.

AND IF YOU PROMISE TO BE MY PERSONAL SLAVE FOR ALL ETERNITY, I WON'T EVEN MENTION IT AT THE PARTY TOMORROW.

SURE. WHATEVER. LET'S JUST GET OFF THIS STUPID GREENBELT.

THIS PLACE CREEPS ME OUT.

REALLY?

>SIGH< YES, KYLE, REALLY.

INTERESTING.

THE SECRET ORIGIN OF CAPTAIN AMAZING.

IT WAS THE BEGINNING OF FIRST GRADE AND I WAS THE LONELIEST GIRL IN THE WORLD.

THEN, ACROSS THE SCHOOL YARD, I SAW THE CUTEST BOY I'D EVER SEEN.

OH! IT'S A LOVE STORY!

HE NEVER SAID MUCH IN CLASS. AND AT LUNCH HE WAS EITHER EATING BY HIMSELF OR GETTING PICKED ON BY BIGGER BOYS.

BUT WHEN HE WAS ALONE, EVERY DAY WAS THE SAME. AFTER HE ATE HIS LUNCH, HE PULLED A LITTLE SLIP OF PAPER OUT OF HIS BAG AND READ IT.

ONE DAY HE DROPPED THE PAPER WITHOUT NOTICING.

I AM A BRAVE BOY. MY HOME IS NEAR.

IT WAS SOOO CUTE. I FELL IN TOTAL, SERIOUS LIKE, Y'KNOW?

TOTAL LIKE. CAN YOU IMAGINE THAT, AMELIA?

NO. I CAN'T.

I MADE IT MY MISSION TO BECOME HIS FRIEND.

AND I WASN'T LONELY ANYMORE.

AND THEN, ONCE YOU GET THE SUPER POWERS, NO ONE CAN BUG YOU ANYMORE. OH, AND I GUESS YOU CAN HELP PEOPLE OR SOMETHING.

YOU HAVE NEAT HAIR

BUT WE DIDN'T HAVE MUCH IN COMMON.

I MEAN, OTHER THAN WE WERE BOTH PRETTY MUCH CONSIDERED LOSERS.

SO I DIDN'T SAY MUCH. I JUST LET REGGIE TALK.

AND WHAT REGGIE TALKED ABOUT WAS *SUPERHEROES*.

HE KNEW ALL THEIR STORIES AND *SECRET ORIGINS*.

I THINK HE WAS WAITING TO BE, LIKE HIT BY A METEOR OR SOMETHING, SO HE COULD BECOME SPACE BOY.

AND HE WAS JUST BIDING HIS TIME, READING THE NOTE HE KEPT WRITING TO HIMSELF.

TRYING TO REMEMBER THAT HE *WAS* A BRAVE BOY, NO MATTER *HOW MANY* BULLIES THERE WERE.

IT WAS MY IDEA TO MAKE THE COSTUME.

I TOLD MY MOM IT WAS A SCHOOL PROJECT, SO SHE HELPED ME MAKE IT.

OF COURSE, HE WASN'T SUPPOSED TO WEAR IT IN *PUBLIC*.

IT WAS JUST TO LET HIM KNOW THAT EVEN IF HE WASN'T A SUPERHERO, HE WAS SUPER TO ME.

THAT'S A REALLY SWEET STORY, RHONDA.

YEAH, WE SHOULD RUN IT IN THE *ZEENIE*.

IT COULD BE A TWO PARTER.

PSST PSST

KYLE! WHAT ARE YOU GUYS DOING HERE?

WE WERE OUT LOOKING FOR STEVES TO TORMENT...

...AND WE THOUGHT WE'D SEE IF YOU GUYS WANTED TO HANG OUT FOR A WHILE.

OOH, COOL! WE'LL BE RIGHT OUT.

LET'S GET DRESSED!

HURRY UP!

SHOULD WE WAKE VIOLET?

SHOULD WE BRING SOME FOOD?

I DON'T THINK THIS IS A GOOD IDEA.

IT COULD BE FUN. BESIDES, WE'RE OUTVOTED.

SHOULD WE HAVE LEFT MARY VIOLET SLEEPING IN THERE?

OH, I'M SURE SHE'LL BE—

BOO!

PTWANG!

EEYAGH!!

DID YOU GUYS GET US OUT HERE JUST TO ACT LIKE A *HORSE'S BEHIND*?

NO, BUT THAT IS A BONUS.

OKAY, SO WHAT ARE WE *DOING* OUT HERE?

WE COULD PLAY A GAME... LIKE GHOST IN THE GRAVEYARD.

OR *SPIN THE BOTTLE*.

NO!

SORRY. *BAD ASSOCIATIONS*.

TRUTH OR DARE?

HMM... DARE!

OKAY.

I DARE YOU...

...TO KISS...

HUH. HERE WE GO!

PAJAMAMAN!

WHAT?

WAIT! WAIT! I—I MEANT TO SAY TRUTH...I... OHH... SHOOT!

can it be on the cheek?

FINE. CHICKEN.

SMOOCH

EEEW! BLECH GROSS!

WHAT DID YOU HAVE FOR DINNER? PEANUT BUTTER AND PASTE?

BLECH

MY TURN. OKAY, UMM...

RHONDA!

OH NO!

TRUTH or DARE?!

AFTER WITNESSING THAT? TRUTH.

OKAY...

ARE YOU, OR ARE YOU NOT, STILL TOTALLY in ♥LOVE♥ WITH REGGIE?

OF COURSE I AM.

DUH, JOAN.

WELL, SHOOT...

...THAT WAS NO FUN!

NOW I GO, RIGHT?

hmm...

KYLE!

TRUTH, BABY. I GOT NOTHIN' TO HIDE.

OKAY. SO, LAST SPRING?

YEAH?

WHEN YOU AND AMELIA PLAYED SPIN THE BOTTLE?

YEAH?

OOOOOH... I AM SOOO *KILLING* HER!

AND YOU GUYS...

Y'KNOW...

...*KISSED?*

YEEEEAH?

How was it?

WELL...

AHEM

I'M GLAD YOU ASKED.

LIKE A PLUNGER ~PWOK~

AND THE BREATH WAS *NOT* MINTY FRESH.

LIKE *MAYONNAISE* AND *KITTY LITTER*.

BUT ENOUGH ABOUT THE *GOOD* POINTS.

LET'S TALK MOISTNESS.

(nice going, *Rhonda*.)

(I was trying to embarrass *HIM*.)

(the boy with no shame?)

(I thought it'd be awkward.)

(mission accomplished)

(I'm sorry.)

WHATEVER.

I GUESS IT'S MY TURN NOW, HUH?

I GUESS SO.

OKAY, THEN, LET'S SEE.

FEEL LIKE *CHICKENING* OUT?

HERE WE ARE.

FEEL LIKE LOSING SOME *TEETH*?

DO YOU KNOW WHAT YOU'RE DOING?

NO.

THIS IS *CRAZY*.

YOU *KNOW* THAT, RIGHT?

I GUESS.

BUT DON'T WORRY. I'M A BRAVE GIRL. MY HOME IS NEAR.

OKAY, YOU RIDE YOUR BIKE TO THE BIG BOULDER...

...PICK UP THE COMIC I LEFT THERE, AND RIDE BACK.

REMEMBER, IT DOESN'T COUNT WITHOUT THE BOOK.

RHONDA? I . . .

NOT NOW.

SHE'S GOING.

GOOD LUCK, AMELIA!

HEY!

WAS THAT GESTURE DIRECTED AT ME?!

THIS IS *NOT* GOOD.

SHE'S TAKING WAY TOO LONG.

NO, SHE'S OKAY. JUST WAIT.

I JUST WISH I COULD *SEE*.

THIS IS ALL <u>YOUR</u> FAULT! YOU TOTAL, UNBELIEVABLE JERK!

<u>MY</u> FAULT?!

IT WAS <u>YOUR</u> STUPID DARE!

YEAH, WELL, WE'LL ALL BE IN TROUBLE IF SOMETHING *HAPPENED*, WON'T WE?!!

THIS IS NOT GOOD.

Against
Unbelievable
Odds

REGGIE, I'M GETTING SCARED.

...UT NOW I REMEMBER, I'M ...ACLEREGGIE

OKAY. JUST WAIT HERE.

WHAT ARE—

JUST WAIT HERE.

POUND POUND FOUND

Reginald?

WHERE'S TANNER?!

Upstairs.

TAAMNNERR!!

What's Wrong?

But worst of all, I know *HE'S* out there.

WHO?

The Shadow man.

He's BEHIND all this.

The rest are just his minions.

IS...IS IT GETTING *DARKER*?

Yes.

It's all his PLAN.

He'll cover the world in *DARKNESS*.

Block out all of the *LIGHT*.

Then, in the *DARK*, he'll come for me.

THEN YOU **HAVE** TO **FIGHT** HIM!

I can't.

Not anymore....

I don't have the HEART.

GET BACK HERE, YOU JERKS! COWARDS!

RHONDA, WHAT'S GOING ON?

WHERE IS SHE?

SHE WENT INTO THE WOODS ON HER BIKE! IT WAS A DARE! SHE'S BEEN GONE REALLY LONG!

Oh No.

GIVE ME THE FLASHLIGHT!

EVERYBODY STAY CLOSE. AND JUST STAY CALM.

WE'RE GONNA FIND HER.

A firefly?

DON'T YOU SEE?

SHADOW MAN WON'T TAKE ALL THE LIGHT AWAY.

HE CAN'T.

Why not?

BECAUSE *SOME* LIGHT COMES FROM *INSIDE*.

THIS IS A SIGN.

WE CAN FIGHT HIM.

WE CAN WIN.

But... I told you, my—

I KNOW.

BUT MINE'S STRONG ENOUGH FOR BOTH OF US.

LET'S GO.

Mom? Mom?
Mom? Mom?

AMELIA?
OH, AMELIA!
THANK GOD!

Tanner?

SHE'S OVER
THERE. SHE
GOT YOU HERE
SAFE.

SHE WOULDN'T
LEAVE YOU. NOT
EVEN FOR A *MINUTE*.

she's not
wearing
Pants.

JUST
REST, HONEY.

I'LL GET
THE DOCTOR.

'Kay.

mom?

YES, HONEY?

I love
you.

I LOVE
YOU, TOO.

IN THE DAYS AFTER THE ACCIDENT, I GOT GOOD NEWS AND BAD NEWS.

I WAS GONNA BE OKAY, BUT I HAD A CONCUSSION. IF YOU'VE NEVER HAD ONE, IT'S KINDA LIKE HAVING YOUR BRAINS SQUEEZED OUT OF YOUR EYEBALLS. NOT FUN.

ON THE PLUS SIDE, ALMOST EVERYONE I KNOW BOUGHT ME A PRESENT.

UNFORTUNATELY, EVERY SINGLE ONE WAS A BIKE HELMET.

BUT I GUESS I SHOULDA SEEN THAT COMING.

HERE'S SOMETHING ELSE WE SHOULD'VE SEEN COMING . . .

WHILE WE WERE PLAYING TRUTH OR DARE, KYLE SENT ONE OF THE OTHER NINJAS OVER TO TRASH OUR CLUBHOUSE.

IT TURNS OUT THAT THE WHOLE LEGION OF STEVES THING WAS JUST SOMETHING KYLE MADE UP TO ANNOY HIS MOM'S BOYFRIEND.

BUT REGGIE IS STICKING WITH IT, AND CAPTAIN AMAZING IS STILL ON AN ANTI-STEVE CRUSADE.

YOU GOTTA SORTA ADMIRE THAT KINDA PERSEVERENCE AGAINST REALITY.

UNFORTUNATELY, HE'S PERSEVERING WITHOUT RHONDA, WHO QUIT SUPERHEROING ALTOGETHER.

I THINK SHE DID IT JUST TO GET REGGIE'S ATTENTION.

AND I THINK IT'S WORKING.

ANOTHER KINDA COOL SIDE EFFECT WAS THAT DAD CAME AND SPENT A WEEK WITH US.

HE SLEPT ON THE COUCH, BUT OTHER THAN THAT, IT WAS LIKE THE OLD DAYS.

WHEN HE LEFT, IT WAS HARD TO SAY GOOD-BYE.

IT TURNS OUT THAT BEFORE SUMMER WAS OVER, THERE WOULD BE AN EVEN TOUGHER GOOD-BYE.

I TALKED TO KYLE. HE DIDN'T KNOW ANYTHING.

HE JUST HEARD SOME RUMOR YOU WERE MOVING.

BUT I TOLD HIM IT WASN'T TRUE.

Oh.

THERE'S A DOCTOR IN CALIFORNIA. HE'S REALLY GOOD WITH WHAT I...

WE'RE GONNA STAY AFTER... EVERYTHING.

AFTER WHAT?

THE OPERATION.

OPERATION?

IS IT SERIOUS?

YEAH.

SORRY. I'M... THAT WAS STUPID. ANYWAY, KYLE FEELS REALLY BAD.

HE TRIED TO APOLOGIZE TO *ME*, TOO, BUT I WOULDN'T EVEN LET HIM.

HE'S NOT WORTH IT, Y'KNOW? HE'S . . .

INSIGNIFICANT.

YEAH...

INSIGNIFICANT.

GOOD WORD.

THANKS.

WELL, I DIDN'T MEAN FOR THIS TO BE A GOING AWAY PRESENT, BUT . . .

IT'S MY AUNT SARAH'S LOCKET.

INSIDE THERE'S A PICTURE. I HAD SAM DRAW IT.

IT'S SUPPOSED TO BE YOU DRESSED AS PRINCESS TRISHARA.

DO... DO YOU LIKE IT?

Thank You.

Thank You.

Thank You.

Oh... SHUT UP.

I SHOULD THINK ABOUT GOING HOME.

YEAH, HEY, IT'S GETTING DARK.

DO YOU NEED MY DAD TO GIVE YOU A RIDE?

NAH. I'LL WALK.

ACROSS THE GREENBELT? ARE YOU SURE?

YEAH. I'M A BRAVE GIRL. MY HOME IS NEAR.

SO I'VE HEARD.

AND THAT WAS THE LAST TIME I SAW HER.

HER FAMILY MOVED AWAY. AND TRISH NEVER WROTE OR CALLED.

THE NEXT *ZEENIE* CAME OUT AND TRISHARA WAS ON THE COVER.

BUT THERE WAS NO STORY INSIDE.

AND THAT STINKS.

WE NEVER FOUND OUT HOW IT ENDED.

Well, what do you want?

Not everything ends with "Happily Ever After."

I mean, sure. I'm a Fairy Princess, so I can tell the future and stuff.

But you wouldn't want that, would you?

Okay. Maybe just a peek.

158

Several Years later...

... IT WAS REALLY GREAT.

DID YOU SEE SUNDAY? HOW IS SHE?

WELL, YOU KNOW SUNDAY. SHE'S TOTALLY CRAZY.

AND WE WOULDN'T WANT IT ANY OTHER WAY.

YEAH.

HEY, RHONDA. I'M GLAD I GOT TO SEE YOU BEFORE THE GAME.

ME, TOO. ARE YOU SURE YOU CAN'T COME?

NAH. TANNER ORDERED PINEAPPLE PIZZA AND GOT A MOVIE. BUT TELL REGGIE I SAID GOOD LUCK.

OKAY.

I'LL CALL YOU WHEN YOU GET BACK HOME.

OKAY, BYE.

BYE.

AMELIA.

A PACKAGE JUST ARRIVED FOR YOU.

A PACKAGE? WHO EVEN KNOWS I'M HERE?

ONLY ONE WAY TO FIND OUT.

HEY, TANNER? THANKS AGAIN FOR LETTING ME STAY HERE.

NO PROBLEM.

IT'S WHAT I DO.

WELL, KEEP UP THE GOOD WORK

The Adventures of
Princess Trishara

Conclusion

FLIP
FLIP
FLIP

The whole kingdom believed Shadowman was dead, defeated in the Woods of Amelora. Princess Trishara knew better. She knew that somehow he was still with her and that she needed to face him alone.

THE SURGERY WAS A SUCCESS.

If she didn't, she would never be free, and one day he would destroy her.

BUT FRANKLY, WE EXPECTED HER TO BE DOING MUCH BETTER.

WE'VE DONE ALL WE CAN. IT'S UP TO HER NOW.

And so, alone, without friends, protectors, or even much hope...

...she reached for her Magic Wand.

"You've taken lots from me," she said. "You almost took it all."

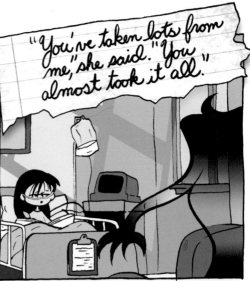

BUT YOU WON'T DEFEAT ME.

BECAUSE I AM A **BRAVE GIRL.**

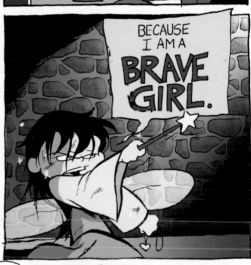

MY **HOME** IS **ALWAYS** **NEAR!**

AND **YOU...**

HSSSSS.

"AND YOU..."

166

AMELIA! LETS GO!

COMING!

But that's all in the future.

HOME SWEET HOME

There's lots between now and then. More school, more play. Lots more laughs, a few more tears.

More friends.

Amelia once said she didn't want to grow up. I wonder if she still feels that way?

I kinda bet not.

As for me?

I can't wait.

Jimmy Gownley's

AMELIA RULES! ™

Join Amelia and the gang for
adventures, mishaps, and homework.

Collect them all!

☐ **#1:** *The Whole World's Crazy*
ISBN: 978-1-4169-8604-1

☐ **#2:** *What Makes You Happy*
ISBN: 978-1-4169-8605-8

☐ **#3:** *Superheroes*
ISBN: 978-1-4169-8606-5

☐ **#4:** *When the Past Is a Present*
ISBN: 978-1-4169-8607-2

☐ **#5:** *The Tweenage Guide to Not
Being Unpopular*
Coming April 2010!
ISBN: 978-1-4169-8610-2 (hc)
ISBN: 978-1-4169-8608-9 (pbk)